I0583806

TOUCHSTONE

SONIA ORIN LYRIS

Knotted Road Press

Touchstone
Sonia Orin Lyris
Copyright © 2016 Sonia Orin Lyris
All rights reserved
Published by Knotted Road Press
www.KnottedRoadPress.com

ISBN: 978-1-64470-169-0

A prequel to *The Seer,* first publication 2016, Baen Books.

Cover art:

Interior design copyright © 2020 Knotted Road Press

It's True. Reviews Help.

If you liked this book, please consider giving a rating and a review. Even a short "Can't wait for the next one!" will do nicely, and help the author to make more books for you.

Never miss a release!

I announce new projects on my Facebook feed.

facebook.com/authorlyris

You can also sign up for my newsletter.

https://lyris.org/subscribe/

Also by Sonia Orin Lyris

The Stranger Trilogy

The Seer

Touchstone

Mirror Test

It Might be Sunlight

The Angel's Share

Blades

Touchstone

POHUT'S younger brother was trembling.

"It's all right, Innel," Pohut whispered to him, though he wasn't at all certain that it was. Why were they here, waiting for an audience with the king? What was expected of them?

"Now," came the sharp voice of the king's pinched-faced seneschal, who pushed the two boys through an opening door.

Inside the room, Pohut struggled not to be distracted by the bright maps on the walls. Before him was the king of the empire, sitting behind a large desk, staring directly at them. In the months they'd lived in the palace with their mother and little sister Cahlen, this was the first time they had been in the monarch's presence.

Innel was already dropping to his knees, grabbing Pohut's hand to tug him down. Pohut went down fast, too fast, wincing at the pain as his knees hit the floor. Both boys touched their foreheads to the wood at the same time.

"You may stand," said the seneschal. When they did not move, he said their names, and then again. This time it was Pohut who drew Innel to his feet.

"Come closer," said the king.

He seemed so large, the king. Which made sense, because the Arunkel empire was huge. Pohut knew how huge, too, because before his father had become a general, he had been a mapmaker.

The brothers shuffled forward hesitantly, stopping when the seneschal held up a hand.

Restarn esse Arunkel, Pohut mouthed silently.

Restarn who is the Empire.

The door shut behind them. The sound echoed.

"Do you know why you're here?" asked the king.

"No, Your Royal Majesty," Pohut whispered, wondering if he'd used the right form of address. He could not seem to think. Tense, he swallowed.

"Your family has been here since—when? Spring? Not quite a half year, then."

"Yes, Sire," Pohut answered uncertainly.

Spring. When they had last seen their father.

"You'll live in the palace," their father had told them after reading the king's letter. "While I go off and take care of this little problem for His Royal Majesty." He had smiled at them, but to Pohut it had seemed forced.

Their mother had looked around the front room of their home. It was early spring and outside the river valley's breezes smelled like life. "Why can't we stay here, Pewyan? Why must we leave at all?"

"It is the king's will, Neleva," his father had said. "To see to it that you're all well cared for. And we can hardly say no. In any case…the palace!" He smiled wide. "Don't you want to see why they call it the Jewel of the Empire?"

Pohut remembered how eagerly he and his brother had nodded.

"You'll study hard," his father had told them. "Make me proud. When I come back, oh, the celebration we'll have!"

Just before he'd left, he'd given Pohut a serious look, hands on his shoulders. "Take care of your mother and brother and baby Cahlen for me. Yes?"

"Yes, papa."

His father had kissed him on the forehead and had left.

And so the family had packed, arranged for the garden, goats, and sheep to be looked after. It was an ache to leave home, to say goodbye to his father, but...the palace! They smiled bravely and let the king's men take them from the only home they'd ever known to the teeming capital city, where the Jewel of the Empire glittered pink and white in the sun, massive and sprawling.

"What have you learned, boy, in the time you've been here?"

Pohut's attention snapped back to the king.

That he was not to wander the palace on his own. That his tutors were often surprised at how clever the brothers were. That he must be very careful in everything he said.

Not the right answers, he was somehow certain. He glanced around for inspiration, eyes falling on the wall-to-ceiling map of the empire, a map he knew his father had helped create. Somewhere there, toward the north and east, his father now fought for the king. This king.

He could remember his father's smile.

"I have bettered my reading and my letters, sire. I have learned to fight."

"Oh, have you?"

Pohut's breath caught as he realized that was not a right answer.

"I have much to learn," he said quickly, thinking of the unadorned canes he and his brother had been given to play with, along with the admonition not to poke each other's eyes out. "If it pleases you, sire."

The king's examination of him made him feel hot. The

king turned the same look on Innel. "And you? What have you learned?"

"That his majesty is generous to the family of—" Innel looked around, eyes wide. "Of General Pewyan, sire. Thank you." He ducked his head, reddening.

Innel must have been rehearsing that while Pohut answered. He felt a flush of pride at his younger brother's smooth answer.

"Fine manners, at least," the king muttered. "Pohut, what do you think of my daughter, Cern?"

Cern, the seven-year-old daughter of the king, the same age as Pohut.

Cern, the heir to the throne.

The brothers had sometimes been allowed to watch the children of the princess's Cohort play, outside, in their fenced yard. He had seen her there, encircled by so many guards and aides that she seemed small.

"She is smart and beautiful," Pohut said.

"Yes, of course she is." The king's tone was a flat irritation.

Pohut swallowed a sudden sick feeling. He'd said the wrong thing.

"I am better at maths," he said. He remembered his mother joking that their father loved maps and numbers more than his own children. Even baby Cahlen, three this next spring, could already count.

The king raised an eyebrow. "You think so?"

Pohut licked his lips and pushed on. He felt as if he were drowning, but could see no way to back out. "I have heard it said she doesn't care for the study."

"Have you indeed? And how is she with the sword? What have you heard about that?"

He had seen pairs of Cohort children divided out into duels, swinging padded sticks. In the center of the yard had been the princess, a ring of guards around her and a miserable-looking boy facing her.

"I don't know, sire," he said. "Everyone was afraid to hit her, so they swung to miss."

At this the king chuckled, and it seemed a very good sound. Pohut exhaled dizzy relief.

"And you, Innel? You like my daughter?"

"Yes, sire. She is very royal."

The king grunted. "All right, enough." Then, tapping the desk, the king's gaze went to the map. Pohut could feel his look change. He felt a chill, like a puff of frozen air.

"Your father was a fine general."

Pohut straightened proudly. "Yes, Your Majesty." Hope leapt inside him as he replayed the king's words; if his father were no longer a general, then he might now be finished with the battles, and coming to take them home.

"Won the battle," the king said. "But got himself killed doing it." His voice went quiet. "Damn it."

Everything seemed very slow now. Pohut found that he had taken his younger brother's hand. Distantly he heard Innel whimper. Maybe because of how tight he was holding, or maybe because Innel already understood what Pohut refused to know. He stared at the king, then around the room, still gripping Innel.

As he stared at the map, Pohut did not know what he felt. From the edge of vision, the red and black and gold of the king's fine clothes seemed to pulse in time with his heartbeat.

"He was a hero," the king said. Then, in a voice that cracked like a whip: "Say it."

"A hero, Your Majesty," Pohut managed past the tightness in his throat.

"Never forget that. Now, go tell your mother."

As they were escorted from the king's offices, Pohut's mind was a fog.

Mother he found himself mouthing, over and over again. *Mother, the king says…*

~

POHUT EXPECTED HER TO SHOUT. Perhaps to scream. Certainly to weep.

She did none of those.

"No," she said calmly. "It is not true."

Her face was white and her hands trembling as she reached forward into the air. At first he thought she reached for him, and he came close, but she was not even looking in his direction. "No," she said again. The shaking hands brushed the air as if pushing aside branches.

Cahlen was sitting on the floor, doing something with her doll. She looked back over her shoulder curiously. "Papa?" she asked.

"But Mother, the king," Pohut tried again. "He says…"

"No!" His mother turned away, gathering the fall of her skirts and walking to the table. She grasped a mug of wine and raised it to her lips, shaking so violently that it splashed onto her light-colored sleeves. She drained the cup, poured another, drank again.

From Innel came an odd, a guttural sound, like a wounded animal.

A weight Pohut did not think he could bear settled on him. He tried to remember the last words his father had said to him. It seemed important. Was it *goodbye*? He did not think so.

Was it Make me proud?

No, it was: take care of the family.

But how?

His mother stood at the mantle of the fireplace. There sat a deep bowl of soil from their home garden where they had grown squash and beans and teardrop lettuce, surrounded by other items. Dried flowers from the meadows. A robin's egg. A branch of new cedar. A rock from the gravel path around their house. A fall of moss from the forest. That was their way, to have a bowl of home always on the mantle, to surround it with offerings to the spirits of the land who made everything grow.

Not something to talk about here. A rude custom, a foolish superstition. Or worse, an attempt at magery. So they kept it covered. She threw the cloth aside, touched the dirt, then touched her face, again and again, in a ritual he had only seen once before, when her mother had died.

Should he try to comfort her? Or pick up little Cahlen, who seemed, strangely, the calmest of the four of them?

Papa, he thought, I don't know how.

THE NEXT MORNING, the king's seneschal arrived.

He gave Pohut's mother a deep bow. "Neleva, honored wife of the late general Pewyan, Protector of the Realm, Seventh of the Great Generals of Arunkel: His Royal Majesty has sent me to express his inconsolable sorrow at the loss of your venerated husband. Be assured the general is being returned by distinguished and dignified escort to the capital and will arrive within the week. I am to inquire, on behalf of His Royal Majesty, on what day you would have the funeral held."

"No day pleases me," she said flatly.

The seneschal nodded again, then gestured Innel and Pohut aside, into the foyer. His voice dropped. "You both will be sworn to the king this afternoon. Wear your best clothes, if you have any. Be certain you are tidy. Do you understand?"

The two boys gave each other a quick, confused glance.

"It is the oath of fealty," the seneschal said. "You offer the king your lives in service to the crown."

"I thought our lives already belonged to the king, ser," Innel said.

"Yes, of course they do," he said, "But to be sworn directly is a greater honor."

"What are we swearing to, ser," asked Pohut, "if he already holds our lives?"

The man's voice became a hiss. "You question this unparalleled honor? Where is your gratitude? Many would be elated to stand where you stand, and arguably more deserving, hero-father or not. I suggest you keep your tongue still and do as you are told."

"Yes, ser," answered Pohut, blushing at the reprimand, ducking his head. "Still, it seems to me—"

"I will send someone to rehearse with you so you don't bungle your oaths." The seneschal frowned. "Though, in truth, it might be a mercy for you if you did." A short exhale and he left.

Pohut found he was shaking. The two brothers walked back into the room where their mother stood at the mantle.

"Mother? We are to give an oath to the king. Do you know what it means?"

She was standing against the mantle, staring distantly.

"Mother?"

Her fingers were buried to the second knuckles in the dirt. If they had been at home, he was sure, she would be outside, hands and feet deep in the soil.

In his mind's eye he saw their home, their garden. It was dying from lack of care. Grief caught in his throat.

"Mother."

"Pewyan," she said softly to the air. "Take me home."

POHUT HAD EXPECTED someone to come to explain the mysterious oath, but when the king's guards arrived, they took the brothers to a large chamber. There the king sat on a huge, raised chair. Beside him stood a handful of adults wearing the royal red and black, with various chains of office around their necks and glinting rings on their fingers.

All eyes were on the two boys.

"Your Majesty," said the woman closest to the king, in what seemed to Pohut a reproachful tone.

"Lismar," the king said in a similar tone, "their tutors say they are very clever. Consider the bloodline. Even you admired General Pewyan's work."

"Clever is not enough, sire," the large man on the king's other side said with a sour look. "One must select one's acorns with care."

"Without nurture, Lason, even the most promising sapling becomes a dead, brittle twig. Let's see how they do when they have plenty of water and sunlight. Who knows? They might take after their father."

A snort from the man called Lason. "Or their mother, who by all reports is…" He grimaced. "Fragile."

"The Houses will rage at the insult," said Lismar.

The king waved this away like a troublesome fly. "If they object, we'll return their precious babies. There are plenty more children. They'll behave."

Lismar chuckled.

Pohut had no idea what this was about. Precious babies?

He realized that these were the king's royal siblings. Lason, he was pretty sure, now glaring at the brothers as if they were a particularly unpleasant mess he had to clean up, was the Lord Commander of the king's armies. His father had mentioned Lismar before. General Lismar.

"Also, I want a close eye kept on the girl-child," said the king. Then he gestured to a short, thickset man to the side, who had a scar jutting up and across his upper lip that made his expression seem puzzled. "Cohort Master, are you ready to induct?"

"Yes, your majesty."

Cohort Master? Induct?

All at once, the pieces fell together, and Pohut understood. His breath came hard.

The Princess's Cohort. Which he had been told was full of the children of aristos and the Houses. Not boys from a remote river valley.

Make me proud.

He drew himself upright. "We are honored, your majesty," he said, forcing words through a drying mouth, hearing his voice crack. "My brother and I are eager to serve you, sire."

"You see?" the king said to everyone. "A rural education, yet behold this skillful comportment. Lismar, read them the oath."

The general did so, from memory, pausing for the brothers to repeat each phrase.

The king passed an ornate knife to the Lord Commander, who passed it in turn to the Cohort Master, who took Pohut's hand in his own. Pohut bit his lip as the knife pricked his palm, but made no sound. The Cohort Master's large hand squeezed three drops onto the bright blade. The king drew Pohut into an uncomfortably close, one-armed embrace. With his other hand, he touched his fingers to the blade, then put red-stained fingertips on Pohut's forehead. The king smelled incense, iron, and sweat. Next, a wide-eyed Innel received the same treatment.

Pohut wasn't entirely sure what he had just sworn to, but understanding came soon enough; they were taken to a small room and directed to write the oath, again and again, until they got it exactly correct, while the meaning and history of each word, phrase, and sentence was explained to them at astonishing length.

After they had inked a final copy onto fine vellum, their thumbs were pricked and the oath was marked in blood, followed by a dire warning about the consequences of failure that left Pohut feeling ill and Innel trembling uncontrollably.

～

THEY WERE ESCORTED to their suite by a handful of king's guards.

"A few things only," one said. "You'll be wearing the Cohort's colors, so you don't need to bring any clothes."

His sister Cahlen wriggled when he picked her up. She had, he now saw, tugged every bit of stuffing out from her doll and carefully arranged it in a circle around the remains of fabric, which lay neatly flattened in the middle. He hugged her tightly to him, hoping to comfort her, but she squirmed silently out of his arms, went to the center of the circle, and with fierce concentration, stomped on the doll's remains, again and again, as if attempting to kill a particularly slow bug.

Pohut looked around the room, trying to figure out what to take. Yet again he was being taken away from somewhere he knew to somewhere he didn't.

Innel was holding himself, tightly, staring at their mother, his expression stricken. Pohut put a hand on his brother's head, forcing himself to smile.

"We'll be fine, brother," he said. "It'll be—fun."

Innel did not look convinced.

"Mother," Pohut said, trying to summon a tone like the one his father had used, when he left home, "the king has taken us into the princess's Cohort." He waited, but she did not respond. "I don't know when we'll be allowed back." A look at the Cohort guardians told him nothing. Hesitantly he reached out and touched his mother's shoulders, as he remembered his father used to do, hoping he was doing it right. "Mother?" He looked where she was looking, but there was nothing there.

Finally he went to the mantle and touched the dirt, touched his face. He examined the items there for a long moment, then took the rock. A plain rock, about the size of his fingertip to first knuckle, brownish and gray, full of messy striations that meant nothing.

That meant home. He put it in his pocket.

At the doorway, he paused. His mother sat at the table, as if frozen. Pohut exhaled heavily, and let the guardians lead them away, as behind him Cahlen continued her slow, silent stomping.

"THE COHORT WEARS the colors of dawn," the Cohort Master said as they stood outside the Boys' Quarters. He made a soft smacking sound as he spoke, the deep scar keeping his lips from meeting quite right. "This signifies your beginning in this illustrious fellowhood. While jewelry and trinkets are acceptable, to wear House colors is not permitted while under the tutelage of his gracious majesty." A sideways look at the brothers. "That will not matter for you."

A liveried servant, a girl perhaps a few years older than Pohut, handed the two brothers a bundle of clothes. They were light blue and pale yellow, secured with a thick cord of red and black.

Pohut wondered what life was like for her. Had she folded these clothes? Tied the cord?

Was her father still alive?

"Thank you," he said to her and smiled.

Her eyes went wide, as if she were shocked that he had seen her. She dipped her head once, cheeks reddening, and left at a near run.

"I don't think you were supposed to do that," Innel said softly.

"I guess not."

The Boy's Quarters was a long, narrow room, with tens of beds lining the walls, some low and some loft, cabinets underneath or to the side. Some boys lounged on the beds, others sat in chairs, some hung off ladders. All watched as the brothers passed by.

The Master led them to a bed where another boy, about Pohut's age, was angrily gathering game pieces and a board.

"You don't need three beds, Mulack," said the Master.

"The Cohort is supposed to be closed," the boy named Mulack muttered, glaring at Pohut and Innel.

"His Majesty's Cohort. If he says it's open, it's open."

Something hard hit Pohut on the back. A block of wood thudded across the floor. A dozen boys returned his look innocently.

"Sutarnan," the Master said, not even turning around, "hitting someone in the back is considered cowardly. Is that the reputation you seek?" He turned to look directly at a smirking boy. "They don't have your advantages, child of the Houses. Give them a few hours' courtesy, at least."

"Never seen them before," Sutarnan responded. "What's their House?"

"No House," said the Master.

"What family, then?" asked someone else.

"Our father is a general," Innel said loudly.

Pohut swallowed at the sudden pain that threatened to claw its way up through his throat into his eyes.

"A hero of the empire," the Master added, "of whom we are all very proud."

"A commoner general," whispered Mulack to another boy with a snort. "In a year, no one will remember his name."

Pohut felt the Master's grip tight on his shoulder an instant before understanding settled into his stomach and face as flashes of heat.

With a humorless smile at Mulack, the Master said, "Careful, ser House Murice, that the same is not said of you."

Mulack, who clearly had not expected to be overheard, took a step backward and looked away.

Scanning the faces of the assembled boys for a long moment, the Master spoke again. "Tokerae, will you help them get settled and see them through the midday meal?"

"Yes, ser," replied a thin, tall boy, who launched himself off his loft bed, foregoing the ladder, landing easily on the floor, bounding forward. He clasped Pohut's arm and grinned. "No House? I've never met anyone without a House before."

TOKERAE LED them to the meal room, where they followed him between tables of children, every one of them watching. Suddenly, someone stuck out a leg in front of Pohut, who barely avoided tripping. Tokerae turned with surprising speed and kicked the leg savagely.

"Ow!" cried the owner of the leg. Mulack.

"Master said to give them a few hours," Tokerae said.

"Turdface," Mulack said. "I'll remember this."

"Doubt it. You forget everything else." Tokerae led them

forward between the tables. A girl stood from her seat to face him.

"Move, sea-scum," he said.

She was a big girl, even measured against Tokerae, and Pohut guessed that she was among the eldest, eight or maybe nine. She had a solidity to her that made Pohut think that she'd move only when she decided to.

"Pestilence and pus," she said in a measured way. "Seems House Etallan has dumped their trash in our meal room."

It took Pohut a moment to realize that this was directed at Tokerae and not the two brothers. He was still half in shock that the children of the nobility were not nearly as polite or gracious as he had imagined they would be.

Tokerae stepped close to the girl, nearly nose to nose. She grinned, eyes flashing.

From across the room, the Girls' Warden called out, in a bored tone. "No fighting in the meal room."

"Come on, Taba," Tokerae said, stepping back, "let us by."

The girl named Taba seemed to consider this, the warden, and the brothers, and she moved aside with a contemptuous snort and watched them pass.

Tokerae's destination became clear: a nearly empty table at the far side of the room, where a young boy and girl sat, both about Innel's age. Their heads were together, laughing at a shared joke.

Something soft but heavy hit Pohut on the back of his leg. He turned to see a clod of straw and mud splattered across the floor.

"Pah!" called Sutarnan, "Animals have found their way into our meal room. They're tracking in dirt! Get them out, wardens!"

"Animal, animal, animal!" shouted a small girl.

"So ugly they hurt my eyes," said Mulack.

"What are they?" asked a younger boy.

"Huge worms?"

"Wrinkled pigs?"

"No, no," replied Sutarnan, choking on laughter. "They are street-dogs!"

"Are you sure?" asked another girl, hair in long braids down her back. "I've seen the king's dogs. They're beautiful. These ones are clearly deformed."

"Mongrels," said Mulack, "slipped in through a chimney or privy hole to steal food." He mimed notching an arrow to a bow, aimed at Innel. "Let's see how they die."

Instinctively, Pohut put himself between his brother and Mulack as they followed Tokerae to the table.

One of the children barked, dog-like. Then another. In a flash, the room was a cacophony of barking and howling. Innel put his hands over his ears.

An ear-piercing whistle cut through the din. The room went silent.

"Enough," said the Cohort Master, standing in the doorway. "Beyond enough. The rest of the meal without voices."

"What? That's not fair," called out the small boy at the table at which they now stood. "I made no sound at all, Master."

"Nor I," said the small girl next to him primly. "I am innocent of all offense."

"Mulack and Sutarnan, you both heard me say a few hours of courtesy. So now everyone will eat in silence except the newcomers and their table. Be thankful I let you eat at all. I may be less generous at dinner, so try to summon a hint of the excellent manners your parents assured his majesty you had in such abundance."

Angry glares fell on the brothers, as if this were their fault.

Tokerae introduced the boy and girl at the table. "Putar of House Kincel," he said. The boy reached out and clasped Pohut's arm in greeting, then Innel's. The girl did likewise. "Malrin, House Eschelatine."

Putar and Malrin seemed wary, but curious. Which, after their general reception, seemed a great improvement.

"Are you from a House, too?" Innel asked Tokerae.

"House Etallan," Tokerae replied. "Most of us are from the Great Houses. Some from the Lessers. A few from the families." A tilt of his head, a smirk. "Then there's you."

Pohut could not tell if this was meant in a friendly way or not. He understood every word spoken, but somehow felt as if it were a different language.

What were they doing here?

THAT NIGHT, returning from the evening meal, the brothers found their lower bed covered with a bucketful of muddy straw and a bloody bone lying in the middle.

"Welcome, mutts!" someone shouted. He wasn't sure who. Sutarnan? Mulack? Ilmach? Dil? He was learning names and Houses as fast as he could. Not fast enough.

Innel was staring at the bed, his mouth slack with shock.

"Pah," Pohut said to him, rubbing his head reassuringly. "It's nothing. Room for us both up top." He pressed his brother toward the ladder.

Once they were both in the loft, Innel toward the wall and away from the edge, Pohut listened to the mutterings and creakings of the room. He felt his brother begin to shake with sobs and rolled him around so he could see his face and whisper in his ear.

"Very quietly, little brother. Show only to me. Never them."

"What are we going to do?"

It was the same question Pohut asked himself. So many unspoken rules. They were not merely outsiders from a strange river valley where everything was done differently. More like mice in an open field, the cry of hawks above.

What *were* they going to do?

Study hard.

"We will study." His answer felt inadequate. "And we will — " Make their father proud, he almost said.

No. Their father was gone. And their mother nearly so.

He gently put his hands on either side of his brother's face and looked into his eyes. "We will study and work hard. We will make each other proud. Together. Always. Understand?"

Under his fingertips, he felt his brother nod. "Always."

THEY STOOD IN OAK HALL, the Cohort's main study. A girl stood next to Pohut, a little older than he was. He drew from his memory of the lengthy introductions.

Sachare of House Nital. He was almost sure.

"Her highness enters last," Sachare whispered to them, out of the blue, as Cern entered. "She is surrounded by guards. Don't ever go up to her uninvited. Also, you only need to bow your head this much, because we are the Cohort. It is the fifth obeisance. You know the forms, yes?"

"No," Pohut said, feeling lost.

"Just dip your head."

"Thank you," Pohut said gratefully.

"Why are you helping us?" Innel whispered. His brother's charming smile, still thick with baby fat, somehow made the question right.

Sachare sighed. "His Majesty, in his great wisdom, put

you here. It is my duty to crown and king to loyally honor his decisions with everything I do."

Again, Pohut understood the words but not the meaning. Was this some new form of mockery? He thought not: she seemed sincere. Studying her face for understanding, Pohut did not notice the princess until Innel hit him urgently. The brothers dipped their heads.

"You are the new ones," Cern said to the brothers.

Was it a question?

"Yes, Your Highness," he replied.

She seemed disappointed. Or puzzled.

At his answer? At the brothers' being here? Before he could think of what else to say, she had walked past, and lessons began.

Every child in the room wore the pale blue and yellow of the Cohort, but they also sparkled with gemstones and chains, earrings and rings, all in the dual colors of their Houses, or bearing the motif of their families.

Pohut felt bare. The two brothers had nothing like that.

Well, Pohut had a rock in his pocket. He touched it to be sure it was still there.

If Cern were puzzled as to why they were here, she was not the only one.

MOST AFTERNOONS, under a winter sun that slipped quickly behind the hills, the Cohort spent in the fenced yard. Exercises included follow-the-leader over bales and barrels, jumping to reach ropes, hanging and swinging. Then they were left to their own whims. Some crouched on the ground with marbles, others ran, played tag, threw balls, tossed disks.

Calls and shouts. Laughter, taunting, conversation.

Pohut huddled next to his brother, their backs to the fence, their breath like smoke in the frigid air.

"I don't understand," Innel said plaintively.

"I don't either," Pohut said. "So we will study and learn." So many looks and touches, nods and jokes that he didn't understand. "And watch everyone," he said. "Watch how they watch each other."

Across the yard, the Boys' Warden's gaze flickered past a laughing Sutarnan, then back again. Sutarnan saw that he was being watched. He paused for a moment in his taunting jabs at the small boy named Putar, until the warden was looking elsewhere, then resumed. It was clear that Putar was trying to get away, but Mulack was also standing close by, blocking Putar's escape and, Pohut now noticed, the Girls' Warden's view.

The boys smiled and laughed and talked pleasantly as if they were all friends, but it was clear Putar only wanted to get away. Finally Putar ducked, wriggled, dropped to the ground, and scrambled through legs, sprinting to a young girl who wore a small black wooden pendant that matched his own.

"Those two," Pohut said to Innel. "The same House. House Kincel."

This was nothing like the world in which they had grown up, the small river valley where they knew everyone, where how well you wielded a pike or halberd or understood maps, or any number of other trades, was what brought you respect. Not your name, not the house in which you were born.

"We must fit everyone to their Houses and families," he said. "We must know it all. And soon."

His younger brother nodded soberly.

～

THEY WERE DROPPED into the world of the Cohort like a pine cone onto a thundering river. Classes were interspersed with small group tutoring sessions that sometimes expounded on the subject, sometimes went elsewhere entirely. The Cohort took in lectures from philosophers and scholars from places as far away as Vilaros, and as royal as the king's sister—Her Grace Lismar Anandynar, Countess Wynn, Duchess Apparent of Kastin, Commander of the Eastern Legions, and Arbiter of Anchlas—whose full title Pohut had made a point of memorizing, but did not yet understand.

Topics were as wide-ranging as the Grandmother Queen's eastern expansion to how the treasury assayed precious metals with slate paddles upon which were scraped lines of gold. They must know these things, they were told. All of them.

And the moment they did, there would be more.

Geography study was a fast-paced game. The Cohort split in teams that moved rugs representing cities, regions, provinces, and tribal lands across a huge room to place them according to shifting rules. Pohut and Innel excelled at this, geography being one of the subjects that the mapmaker's sons knew well, but when the rules changed again to include political alliances and economic priorities, the brothers flailed, struggled, and were taken aside for more tutoring.

They applied themselves to the extra sessions on subjects the others had apparently been studying since they were able to crawl. Centuries of empiric history. The royally granted House Charters. Sigils, flags, colors. The seven—or was it eight?—different types of obeisance and for whom and when they must or might be used. A bewildering array of court dances. Most importantly, the royal star dance, which required a confusing subtlety of posture and footwork that looked easy until they tried it.

Sword-fighting practice, which meant padded, sword-shaped sticks, with blunted tips on which they were strongly advised not to become overly reliant. His arms ached.

And then, also: which cups and prickers to use with which dinner courses, which made no sense at all.

~

HEAD SWIMMING from a lecture on the House Charters, Pohut stood outside Oak Hall during a short break. Sutarnan stepped up next to him.

"This must all be so strange for you," the other boy said, staring intently at Pohut, "Are we strange to you, too?"

"Yes," Pohut admitted, wondering if the other boy was mocking him or genuinely curious.

"Why are you here, then?"

It was an excellent question, but as he pondered possible answers—his father's death, the king's words—he still did not know. In the Cohort, though, uncertainty was weakness. That he knew.

"To study alongside the princess," he said, summoning what he hoped was an arrogant, confident tone. "Isn't that why we're all here?"

"That's what you think? It's so much more. The possibility of marriage. Then children. She's expected to choose a mate from among the Cohort."

A mate? Marriage? Pohut's mind spun. "You mean we could..? *I* could...?"

Sutarnan barked a loud laugh. "Well, no. Not you. Not mongrels. You understand. She couldn't."

Of course not them. Pohut felt foolish and angry at once. "Then—" why *were* they there? He could not ask that, not of Sutarnan, who he knew would be happy to see them fail "—then why are there girls in the Cohort?"

Sutarnan gave him a pitying look. "Because she'll be the

monarch, you idiot. Remember the Grandmother Queen? Her highness will need advisers, ministers, military leaders. People she knows. Who she can rely on."

"Oh."

"You really don't know much, do you?"

Anger quickened his breath. Hand in his pocket, he gripped the stone, felt himself ease.

"The king put us here. It wasn't our choice."

"Well then, ask to be released from your vows. Tell the Cohort Master you don't want to be here. When the Cohort started last year, there were fifty of us. Now there are barely forty. That's what happened to the others."

It had not occurred to Pohut that it could be easy to leave. Then they could go back to how things had been before.

No, they could never go back. Their father was dead.

"And in truth, that would be good," Sutarnan continued, "because no one wants you here."

Make me proud.

Pohut drew himself up, met Sutarnan's unpleasant smile. "But we *are* here, and we are not leaving."

For a long moment, they stared at each other. Sutarnan broke the look first, laughed, and danced away.

Pohut rubbed the stone in his pocket and watched him go.

EVERY DAY BROUGHT some new unpleasantness on top of the insults and threats. Torn sheets and missing blankets. Eviscerated rats, their entrails spread across their beds. The two boys gave up the lower bed entirely.

Tonight, as they returned from the play yard and evening meal, the stink reached them many steps away. Not the scent of horse or cow dung, either, but the excrement of a predator.

Dog, most probably.

Brown was smeared across every step of the ladder, and Pohut did not want to guess at how bad it would be up top. For a moment they simply stared. Then he took Innel's trembling hand and went to the Master.

"Thought I smelled something," he said when the brothers told them. "What are you going to do about it?"

This Pohut had not expected. "We thought you would tell us, ser."

"Not for me to say, boy. You're the Cohort. Studying to be leaders of the Empire. Make decisions."

Retribution was tempting, if he could be certain who had done it. Mulack? Probably.

But even so, what to do? Pohut suspected that if it came to blows with the children of the Houses, he'd be hit harder than all the play fighting he'd done in his home village had prepared him for.

"Are we going to have to actually fight them, ser?" Pohut asked the Master.

"Probably, sooner or later." His look at the brothers turned sympathetic. "Be sure you can win a thing before you start it."

That sounded like wisdom.

"We'll need water and soap," Innel said, and Pohut's heart warmed at this show of practicality. He might tremble and cry, but Innel thought things through.

"I'll have it sent for," the Master said, instructing servants.

Innel spoke again. "Ser, it doesn't seem fair that we should have to clean up a mess someone else made."

The Master sucked air through the gap in his lips and looked thoughtful. "Let's give you some company, then."

A TENCOUNT and more of servants poured into the hall, toting buckets, soap, and linen rags. The Master walked the length of the long room, repeatedly dipping a wand into a large jar held by an assistant, dribbling honey onto the steps of each loft bed, over increasingly loud objections.

"All this cleaned up," he said as he went, smiling as if he were enjoying himself, "by the next meal, or there won't be one."

When he arrived at Mulack's bunk, Mulack stood in front of his ladder, scowling.

"No."

All grumbling and outrage fell silent. The Master smiled wider, made a gesture, and the Cohort guardians lifted Mulack and set him down to the side.

"My father is the Eparch of House Murice," Mulack shouted, "and I will not scrub and wash like some scullery boy."

The Master stared at him a moment, then turned slowly, meeting the gazes of the boys clustered around. "Consider," he said, "the history of the Cohort. The previous one, as I'm sure you know, included his Royal Majesty and his royal siblings. You might not know that I was privileged to serve as warden. I'm sure you don't know that I have endured every threat you can imagine, and many you can't." He held his arms out and smiled widely. "Behold, I remain."

He let that sink in before he continued.

"You are entirely correct, ser House Murice," he said to Mulack, "that I can't force you to comply with my instructions. But." He stepped up very close to Mulack. "I can send you back to your parents."

With that, the Master sauntered on, applying the honeyed wand more liberally. When he was done, every ladder except the brothers' was pasted with sticky honey, and some of the beds as well.

But the looks the two of them were getting now were far from friendly. Despite that this was not their doing, they were being blamed. Next time, Pohut resolved, they would find their own justice.

While the honey was nothing like the dog dung the brothers now set to addressing, Pohut felt some satisfaction in sharing the work.

And, he realized, it wasn't anything they hadn't done before, tending to their own animals and livestock. He chuckled at the thought that one of the few things the brothers knew how to do that the others did not was to clean up shit. He gave a wry smile to his brother, who smiled back.

THE COHORT ASSEMBLED in a large ballroom, waiting for something to begin. Rhetoric, knot-poetry, dance—Pohut wasn't sure.

"Her Royal Highness," the Cohort Master announced loudly, standing aside from the door. "Princess Cern Anandynar of Arunkel, Pinnacle of the Karmarn and Pelapa, High Consul of Mirsda, and Ur-Kacika of Gotar."

By now Pohut had very nearly memorized Cern's titles. Heads dipped and raised as she passed by. When she was near, Mulack held something out to her: a small, red lacquered horse. She took it with an expressionless nod and handed it to one of the many attendants who always surrounded her.

Next was Sutarnan who held out a small box from which she drew a wreath of tiny, cleverly woven red and black roses, to which she responded similarly.

"Tok," Pohut whispered. "Were we supposed to have a gift?"

"Everyone's parents sent messengers yesterday. Not yours, I guess?"

Child by child, Cern moved down the line, collecting small items.

"You simply spin it, Your Highness, like a top." A boy named Fadrel now dropped to the floor and gave a sharp twist to a small object. "Do you see how the black and white turns to colors?"

An audible inhale from the princess. "Red. Blue. But how is this done? It is not magery, surely?"

"No, of course not, Your Highness," said the Cohort Master sharply, snatching the spinner from the ground and thrusting it backward into the hands of one of his own aides. "But we will have it checked, just to be sure." He gave Fadrel a harsh look.

"It's only a trick," Fadrel muttered hastily, backing away.

More gifts came to Cern as she made her way into the room. A pale pink-and-gray seashell from Taba. From Sachare, a set of cherrywood wands fastened with silk that, shaken, produced a sonorous tinkling.

The princess paused in front of the brothers, stared at them. "You are still here," she said.

Their heads dipped. "Yes, Your Highness."

She looked them up and down, as if trying to figure something out.

Or perhaps she was waiting for a gift.

Pohut felt himself redden. "We didn't know. We don't have anything." Didn't have a family to give them what they needed, to tell them when they needed it.

She nodded, walked on.

They did not belong here, that was clear. Pohut turned Sutarnan's words over in his mind. Could they really leave?

Could leaving the Cohort be as easy as asking? Somehow he doubted it.

～

THE COHORT MASTER SPOKE. "The winter solstice is nearly upon us. Who knows the tradition of the king's solstice cakes?"

"My mother the Eparch had one last year," said Larmna proudly.

"It is a rare privilege, reserved for the king's most favored. The cakes, made by the king's own chef, are thick with the finest wine-soaked fruits from Apapur-Selsane, encrusted with pecans from the Spice Islands. Half the cake is heavily glazed with bright, sweet orange, the other side dusted with the dark Perripin cacao. You could eat at the palace your entire life and taste nothing so wondrous as a solstice cake."

The Master had fallen silent, his lips opening and closing with a soft smacking sound. It seemed that he had forgotten he was talking to a room full of children. After a long moment, the Girl's Warden pointedly cleared her throat.

"Truly magnificent," the Master said, still working his mouth. "In a gesture of extraordinary generosity, the king has informed me that the members of the Cohort shall each be given a solstice cake."

Sounds of delight, whispered exultations.

"And here they are."

Two servants entered, carrying a crate, out of which the wardens began to distribute small, square wooden boxes.

"You are being treated as adults in this. The cake is not to be eaten until midnight on the solstice, demonstrating your ability to stand the privations of winter and thus to be worthy of the bounty of the coming seasons. Hence the coloration of the cake itself, you see? I advise you to treat this honor with the faith that the king vests in you. Restraint is a test of your growing maturity."

The small box Pohut now held was of finely crafted rosewood with the monarchy's sigil carved into it, sealed with wax and the king's mark. The box alone was a treasure.

Across the room, the children were unusually quiet as they each examined their cake boxes.

As he ran a fingertip over the king's seal, Pohut found inside himself a growing awe. He now owned something rare. Priceless, even. He felt more important, merely by holding it.

As he looked around at the children of the Houses and families, eyes sparkling and grinning, he felt something like kinship.

"TODAY BEGINS THE NEXT GAME," The Cohort Master said at the end of the morning meal. "I shall explain the rules."

"We know the rules," interrupted Mulack. "Just tell us the prizes."

Pohut was no longer shocked at this rudeness to an elder, but it still felt wrong. The Master seemed unperturbed.

"The rules change, ser House Murice, as do the players." Glances at the brothers. "The Cohort would not, typically, be invited to the great solstice feast. The princess will be there, of course, as well as most of your families. But not you."

Not the brothers' family, Pohut was certain.

Whispers around the room faded to silence as, one by one, children realized what he was about to say.

"Have your attention now, do I?" He grinned widely, yellowing teeth unevenly revealed where his scar tugged his lip upward. The smile vanished. "Four teams of no fewer than nine. The team that finds the iron bell will sit at the far end of the hall with the captains. The bronze bell places you in the middle, with the aristo families. And whoever finds the silver bell will sit at the royal table, with His Majesty and Her Highness the Princess, in full view of the entire hall."

"I will have that prize," whispered Tokerae fiercely.

"How long do we have?" Fadrel asked.

"The game is over at noon on solstice day, bells found or not," said the Master.

Six days hence.

"Then… lessons are suspended?"

The Master turned a sneer on the asker. "Nothing is suspended. Life does not pause to make way for your opportunity. All lessons, practices, and tutoring sessions continue. You may sleep and eat, though others will doubtless be searching while you do."

"But the palace is huge! It will take forever!"

"Limit yourself to the old palace only. The bells are not behind locked doors. If you break into anywhere, you will have solstice dinner with the pigs."

"You wouldn't," said Mulack.

"Ah, ser House Murice. Shall we find out? "Mulack did not answer. "And a new rule: you will decide your teams. Beginning now."

Barely a blink passed for this to be absorbed by the older children. A flurry of motion filled the room. By the time Pohut understood, an instant later, children were launching themselves across the room toward each other. Shouts and hisses, angry threats, reminders of debts owed.

Mulack was with Sutarnan. Tokerae was sprinting by, and Pohut reached out to grab his arm. Tokerae yanked it back. "I'm not teaming with *you*," he hissed. "I mean to win." And he was gone.

A blink later, the Master's whistle sounded. "Three teams

are now full. The fourth is the remainder." His gaze settled on Pohut. "Pohut, the fourth team is yours."

"Mine?" Pohut squeaked in surprise.

In moments, Putar, Malrin, Larmna, and the rest of the younger and thus unchosen children had come to Pohut's side, looking up at him for direction.

The other three teams were already gone from the room.

NO BELLS WERE FOUND that day, nor the following. When some children didn't show for the required sessions, the Master halted everything until they were found and brought back.

Meals and sleep, on the other hand, were skipped with abandon. Cohort siblings took food back to their quarters and slept in their clothes.

"Is your team even looking?" Sachare asked Pohut as they waited in Oak Hall for the guardians to hunt down an errant child.

Pohut brought to mind what he knew about her House. Nital was aligned with Helata, which might explain why she was on Taba's team.

Or maybe they just liked each other. His head swam.

"We have a plan," he said, summoning a confident tone.

Not much of one, though. His plan was mostly to avoid making things worse.

AT MIDNIGHT, everyone was woken by a loud clanging. Cohort siblings lined the hallway along with the Master in his bedclothes, the wardens, handfuls of guardians. The Master's voice carried.

"The bronze bell has been found. Well done, Tokerae. Your team will join the solstice feast."

Only the winners cheered.

The brothers huddled close in the yard, their breath a pale fog in the dark of late afternoon, watching. Tokerae's team strutted and bragged and clustered together as they had not before, again and again telling how they had found the bronze bell behind a tapestry in the Swan Room.

"We aren't searching very hard," Innel pointed out.

"We aren't searching at all, brother," Pohut agreed. "I think we would not make any friends by winning."

He watched the motion of the children in the yard, the alliances and enmities, some changing quickly, some constant. It was starting to make sense.

Mulack and the small boy called Donal, for example, were both from House Murice. Not close in age or temperament, yet they never fought each other. Tokerae, who did not actually seem to dislike Taba, was nonetheless at odds with her in what now seemed to Pohut a rather perfunctory way, which he concluded was because of their Houses' longstanding feud.

Then there was age: if nothing mattered more, older kids banded together, as did the younger ones. Likewise, the girls were often together.

Except when, as in the case of Taba, House concerns overrode.

He could almost see the lines of connection around him, the forces of opposition. The overlapping, shifting circles of loyalty and tension.

And what was it all for?

Just then Cern walked into the yard. Children made way, eddying and swirling about the mass of guards and aides that encircled her, like a school of fish around a large turtle. If the point of the Cohort was the princess, and all this work was to impress her, Pohut had to wonder: was it working?

He could find no clues in Cern's face, though he tried. What did she think? What did she want?

"When do we start looking?" asked Malrin.

Pohut doubted there was any point, but as he looked down into the girl's eager eyes, he saw one. "Tonight," he said warmly.

Malrin bounced up and down. Eagerly, or to keep warm in the dark and cold, he wasn't sure.

POHUT FOUND it liberating to walk the halls of the palace and go where he liked, which the brothers had been forbidden to do before, even if he were trailed, like a mother duck, by the youngest of the Cohort, and behind them a pack of guardians to keep them out of trouble.

It was a curious feeling, to walk where he liked, to see what interested him. As they strolled, he asked the children of his team about themselves, and began to know them, and through them, their parents, their families, their Houses.

As they went, Larmna began to hum a tune. Putar and some of the other children laughed.

"It's the Finding Song," said Malrin to Pohut's confusion. "The song you sing when you've lost something!"

"We'll teach it to you!" cried Larmna. The others began to clap to keep time, and Larmna sang the simple lyrics. The song asked questions. Have you looked high? Have you looked low? Have you looked inside? And what about on top?

They entered a large study with an otter carved into the heavy door.

"Look!" called Putar, pointing at heavy tapestries. He ran to them, searching among the folds for a way to get behind.

"The bells won't be there," Pohut said.

"How can you know that?" Putar asked, glancing back from his burrowing behind the heavy drapes.

"Because the Master has already done that. He won't do it twice." A hunch, but he was sure.

They searched anyway, and Pohut waited patiently. Then more walking, more singing. They came to the great library where walls of books, scrolls, and lengths of knot-poetry climbed so far overhead that ladders were needed to reach them. A guardian reminded the children that each tome was near priceless, and they should act accordingly.

"I didn't know there could be so many," Innel whispered to him.

Their father had had a collection of books, but this many was beyond imagination. By any measure, the library was astonishing.

"We'll come back," he told his brother. When they were done pretending to look for the bells.

But the bells wouldn't be here either, he suddenly realized. Not behind any one of these thousands of books. Tens of thousands. He said as much.

"And how can you know *that*?" Malrin asked.

"The Master wouldn't want us touching them all," he said.

That wasn't quite it, though. It was this: if a bell were hidden here, finding it would simply be a matter of searching —days or even months—and Pohut was somehow certain that wasn't how the Master thought.

Dil had said that the bronze bell had been hanging on a cord, a tug all that was needed to liberate it. Not only that, Dil said proudly, but it had been his idea to look there, because the tapestry had depicted minstrels playing for a star dance and the minstrel in the center was holding a bell. The bells were not just hidden. They were hidden with clues.

Pohut fidgeted with his rock as he considered. The rock, he saw, was changing color slightly, as the oils of his fingers darkened the tan and gray. It made him think of home.

WHEN HIS TEAM returned from searching, as he was about to climb to the loft to bed, Putar ran to him, shoulders heaving, gulping air, struggling to hold back tears.

"They took our cakes," he said, his voice breaking. "All of the team's cakes. Gone."

Pohut stormed the length of the boy's quarters in a fury, saying nothing, but searching the faces of every boy he passed. He paused at Mulack, looking into his eyes. Was that a flicker of smug cruelty he saw there, or did he only imagine it?

Pohut was finding it easier and easier to see the worst in everyone. And that, he realized, was a kind of blindness.

He comforted the younger children as best he could. Could they search for the cake boxes, they wanted to know. Yes, he replied, but they would not find them, certainly not before the solstice.

Never, he suspected. They could be anywhere. Behind the books in the library.

Or outside the palace, even. Perhaps the parents of the other Cohort children might not think the mutts' were worthy of such an honor.

There was no going to the Cohort Master this time, nor could he take on those who he suspected of the theft. Not until he was sure he could win.

SOLSTICE WAS A DAY AWAY. Mulack and Sutarnan's group, still searching, were sallow from lack of sleep, barely eating.

"Give us a clue," Mulack demanded hoarsely of the Master.

Pohut was beyond being surprised at this rudeness.

"No," said the Cohort Master, curtly, without any humor.

"But we might not find them in time!"

"Oh, I don't think the tables will be hard to fill, ser House Murice, even at the last minute."

"But—" Mulack sputtered, glaring around the room wildly. "That's not fair!"

Pohut suppressed laughter. He leaned in close to Innel and whispered. "Do you see, brother, how lack of sleep makes him even more stupid? There is a lesson for us both."

From outside the room, sharp, urgent shouts followed another clamorous bell-ringing. A glance around the room to see who was missing told everyone it was Taba's team.

Sutarnan scowled furiously at Mulack, as if it were his fault, and stormed out after the Master. Mulack threw down his napkin and followed.

While the rest of the room streamed out to hear the news, Pohut and Innel calmly finished their meal.

WHEN THE BROTHERS went to sleep, Mulack and Sutarnan's beds were empty, their team still out searching. They were back by predawn, when Pohut went to find the privy. On his return to the quarters, he saw a familiar figure in the hallway, carrying a basket. The servant girl.

"Hello," he said to her.

This time she met his look squarely, silently flicking her

gaze to the side and back. Then she turned in that direction and walked away.

Pohut followed. She turned right at the main hallway, walking the length of the wing to the Great Hall where the solstice feast was to be held that night. She stole a quick glance at him before dropping her head then dashing away.

All at once Pohut knew where the silver bell must be. The bronze bell—the middle prize—had been found at eye level, hanging behind a tapestry. The iron bell, which Taba had found the night before—the least of the prizes—had been on the floor of a closet in a supply room, buried under bags in which were stored dancer's bells and keep-time rattles.

He opened the door of the Great Hall and slipped inside. The room was massive, wide and very long, high-ceilinged, with multiple balconies and windows now letting in the pale light of dawn. But the clue was now clear in his mind, so he looked at the balcony where the musicians would play.

There, staring back, wide-eyed, was a face he recognized.

"No, no, no." Donal shouted. "Get out!" The boy stretched his arm out over the balcony railing, reaching for something that was up and behind the rafters, out of Pohut's sight, past a set of hunting horns attached to the wall. In the silence of the hall, Pohut could hear the boy's heavy breathing as his fingertips strained to reach something. Then the very faint sound of metal against wood. Had Donal's arm been just a bit longer, Pohut suspected, he'd have the bell now.

He'd been right, but minutes too late. He was surprised to be disappointed.

Donal looked back at him with a panicked expression. He pulled himself up onto the balcony railing to get closer to his goal, struggling to keep his balance. A step forward, hands groping for something to hold onto, but there was nothing. He lurched for the hidden bell, now in reach, and slipped. Arms windmilling to try to catch himself, Donal went over the railing and fell to the stone floor below, giving a cry that ended suddenly with a hard thud.

One part of Pohut's mind raced to strategy: the bell was now his. He must simply take it before anyone else did.

Now it was easy to imagine himself and his brother sitting at the royal table. With the king. With the princess. That would show the Houses, the aristos, that General Pewyan's sons were of consequence.

He could have it. For a moment, nothing seemed more important.

But in that moment, another part of his mind had already taken over his body. He was already there, gently lifting the limp Donal, running his way back to the Cohort Master.

THE COHORT MASTER took the boy from Pohut and said, "go," then called for aides and the physician.

Pohut thought fast, sprinted back into the Boys' Quarter, and rushed up Mulack's loft ladder. He doubted he would have reached the top if Mulack had not been so dead-tired. Even so, Mulack sat up abruptly, rings of dark around his eyes from lack of sleep, eyes full of hostility.

"I have the bell," Pohut said quickly, seating himself out of range of a swift kick that would send him flying off the bed. "And I will sell it to you," Pohut added.

"Sure you will. What for?"

"Three things. One: the cakes returned."

"Pah! What makes you think I have them?"

"Never mind. Maybe Tokerae has them. Or Taba. I'll go ask them." He made as if to leave.

"No, no, stay. What else?"

Pohut hadn't actually thought that far. It had all happened too fast. Donal. The bell. This plan. "You stop beating up the younger kids. For at least—" What would Mulack agree to? He wasn't sure. "A month."

Mulack smirked, but nodded. "And third?"

Seeing Mulack's expression, Pohut realized he should have asked for more time. Too late now. "One of your rings, to be sure you'll keep your word. I'll give it back at the end of the month."

Mulack snorted. "What if you're lying to me, you don't really have the bell, and now you have my ring, too?"

A good question. Pohut considered as if he were Mulack. "You're stronger than me," he said. He doubted it, but Mulack would think so. "And you have many friends and I have none." He shrugged. "Just take it back."

Mulack nodded. "All right. But why not keep the bell for yourself?"

Because it had come clear to Pohut that the brothers needed more time in the Cohort before they could afford to win such a prize. Time to make friends where possible, and build alliances where not. Until then, to sit at the royal table by the princess and king would, oddly, put them farther behind. The cost of this victory would be too high.

But Mulack wouldn't understand that, he realized.

"You were right," Pohut said. "We're mongrels. We wouldn't know what to do, sitting at the royal table. We don't want to embarrass the Cohort." A humbling lie, but he could stomach it. For now.

Mulack pondered, seemed to find this plausible. He pulled off a ring, held it out on his palm, toward Pohut. "I accept your terms."

A formal contract. This Pohut hadn't expected, but of course he should have; the children of the Houses would know how to make binding contracts, though he had never done such a thing before.

Pohut put his hand palm down atop Mulack's and their hands turned together, so that the ring was left in Pohut's outstretched palm.

"Our contract is made," Mulack said.

Pohut examined the etched silver ring. Inset was a glinting purple stone surrounded by two white ones. The colors of House Murice.

He told Mulack where the bell was.

THAT MORNING AT THE MEAL, everything had changed. No one was looking for bells any more, certainly, not since Mulack had raced out of the Boys' Quarter, returning to ring the silver bell, loudly and for a very long time, even after the Cohort Master had told him he'd won.

As for Donal, the Master refused to say anything beyond that the boy was being sent home to recover. Would not say from what, or whether he would come back to the Cohort. From the surrounding chatter, Pohut learned that Donal was not the first of the Cohort to go home with injuries. The Cohort might have started with fifty, as Sutarnan had said, but not all of them had left willingly.

Perhaps none.

"We must become very strong and very clever, brother," he whispered to Innel. "We must watch out for each other, because no one else will."

"Always," his brother said.

There were other differences that morning. A small nod from Mulack as he walked by. The surprised looks from those who noticed the ring on Pohut's hand. Mulack was silent on the topic, but happy to brag about how clever he was to have found the bell, and how proud his parents would be to see him sitting at the royal table.

The children of Pohut's team were mournful at their run of bad fortune, but they cheered up when, after the meal, they found their solstice cake boxes returned to their cabinets.

Pohut and Innel's boxes, however, had broken seals. Inside were only crumbs.

He went searching for Mulack, stepped up very close. "We had a contract."

He expected Mulack to sneer at him and tell him that the mutts weren't worthy of a contract with a child of the Great Houses, to which he would say... well, he wasn't sure yet. To his surprise Mulack simply nodded. Was that a look of remorse?

"I should have told you," Mulack admitted. "Already eaten when we made the contract. I had to know if they were as tasty as the Master said."

"But that's bad luck!"

"Well, I didn't eat *mine*," said Mulack. He shrugged. "You have the boxes. Just pretend. No one will look carefully if you hide your mouth." He mimed eating behind his hand.

Pohut growled deeply in the back of his throat. Like a dog.

Mulack took a step back. "I didn't mean to. Tell you what —I'll lay off the younger kids for another month past what we agreed—a whole two months!—and keep Sutarnan away, too. All right?"

Pohut wanted to hit him, wanted it badly, but instead thrust a hand in his pocket and gripped the rock tightly.

"I accept your terms," he said.

POHUT LOOKED around at the others of his team, sitting in a small room off the second scullery near the Great Hall. Coming through the walls was the deep booming of drums, the strains of brass horns, and the muffled sounds of a thousand happy, feasting voices, laughing and cheering. Dancers, musicians, jugglers—the show was said to be spectacular.

Of course, Pohut's team was not to be there, and the guardians at the doors would make sure they didn't even try. Glum faces looked back at him.

"If we'd won, we'd be in there now," said Malrin.

"The big kids always win," muttered Larmna.

Pohut felt a longing to tell them what had happened, how they really had won, but no: Mulack would keep this secret, and so must Pohut.

"It's not so bad," he said. "We could be eating with the pigs." There were some chuckles. "You know what I think? That next time, I want every one of you on my team."

Reluctant and shy smiles came his way.

"We still have our cakes," Innel said brightly. Pohut smiled at his brother, proud of him for keeping up the pretense that their boxes were not empty.

Putar opened his mouth wide and mimed eating the entire cake at once, cheeks puffed out.

"But we'll wait until midnight," Pohut said, "so that we have the best fortune of the solstice. And we will have it, too, beginning tomorrow."

Tomorrow, when the younger children would find Mulack and Sutarnan quite a bit more pleasant.

"I wish we had found a bell," Larmna said to him, "but I'm glad we found you, and you found our cakes back again." Nods all around. Malrin began to hum the Finding Song, and Putar began to clap.

Then the door opened, the sounds of the feast

momentarily loud, and they fell silent. Sachare entered, came to the brothers, put a hand on each of their shoulders.

"Come with me," she said softly.

Bemused, they followed her out the side door, past the guardians, who, oddly, did not object, into a small chamber, a tiny side room. The door closed behind them, and one of Cern's attendants, an older girl, glowered down at them. "You will say nothing of this. Not a word." Then she opened the door. In came Cern.

Innel inhaled sharply. They both dipped their heads. In a private room, with the princess. What did it mean?

"I don't have long," she said to them, "before I'm missed. So don't waste my time. Tell me why you gave the bell to Mulack." Pohut's mouth fell open in surprise. Her lips twitched in a humorless smile. "I am told things all the time, and most of them are lies. But this I know: you traded away the silver bell. No one else in the Cohort would have done such a thing. I want to know why."

"Your Highness," Pohut said, stuttering. "If we sat at your table..." How to finish the sentence?

"No one would like us," Innel said. "Even more than they don't like us now."

"Yes," Pohut continued. "At least for now. Next year, it might be different." Then, under his breath, "It *will* be different."

Cern appeared to consider, then gestured to her attendant. "There aren't supposed to be any extras, but..." She handed them two solstice cake boxes, seals intact.

Pohut blinked, trying to reason through what this implied. That they had her attention and her favor, yes, but only for a moment. She turned to go. He thrust a hand into his pocket.

"Your Highness, we have something for you. A solstice gift."

She turned back. He held it out to her.

"A rock?" she asked disbelievingly, looking at the stone, then back at the brothers. "You have seen the presents I receive," Her expression darkened. "Do you insult me?"

"No, no," he said quickly. "Not at all. This rock is special. It…we…" He swallowed hard.

"It's not even pretty," she said.

That was true. So true. How to explain?

"It comes from our home," Pohut said.

"We miss our home so much, Your Highness," Innel said, his high voice so sad it tugged at Pohut.

"It doesn't make color or sounds," Pohut admitted. "It is what it is and nothing else. The other gifts you receive— those beautiful things—they are given to you because they are so precious, all by themselves."

"Of course," she was bemused, bordering on irritated. "So?"

"So," Pohut said, summoning the courage to meet her eyes. "We give you this, because it's that precious to us." He raised his hand a little and held his breath. Would she understand?

She looked away and he thought he'd made a mistake, but then she looked back, nodded and took the rock from his hand. Relief flooded him.

From the hall beyond came sounds of wild cheering as some act concluded. As if in response, from the door they had entered, came the sounds of his own team clapping, high voices loudly singing the Finding Song.

Cern's eyes flickered between the two brothers. "I believe I understand now," she said.

For a moment Pohut had no idea what she meant. Then, suddenly, he did. She meant the reason the king had brought them into the Cohort. Across months and years to come, he would remember those words.

As he watched her leave, his rock gripped as tightly in her hand as it had been in his, Pohut felt an ache pass through him. A weight seemed to ease.

He smiled at his brother, who held the cake boxes.

"I think it's midnight."

Want More?

Read Chapter One of *The Seer*

Purchase *The Seer*, which follows *Touchstone*

Get *The Stranger Trilogy*, sequel to *The Seer*

About the Author

Sonia Orin Lyris's stories have appeared in various publications, including *Asimov's SF magazine*, *Wizards of the Coast* anthologies, and *Uncle John's Bathroom Reader*. She is the author of THE SEER, an epic fantasy novel from Baen Books. Her writing has been called "immersive," "ruthless," and "unsparing."

Her passions include martial arts, partner dance, fine chocolate, and the occasional human critter.

She asks questions and gives answers, but not necessarily in that order. She speaks fluent cat.

A note from Sonia

Thank you for being part of my creative process. I have regular chats for subscribers, on my Patreon account, here:

https://www.patreon.com/lyris

Never miss a release!

I announce new projects on my Facebook feed.
facebook.com/authorlyris
You can also sign up for my newsletter.
https://lyris.org/subscribe/

Connect with Sonia

Web: https://lyris.org

![facebook icon] facebook.com/authorlyris
![goodreads icon] goodreads.com/Sonia_Orin_Lyris
![twitter icon] twitter.com/slyris

www.ingramcontent.com/pod-product-compliance
Lightning Source LLC
Chambersburg PA
CBHW050159110726
47898CB00008B/2862